Same

Kind

of

People

By: Janace L. Griffin

To order additional copies of this book, contact:
Xlibris
844-714-8691
www.Xlibris.com
Orders@Xlibris.com

ISBN: 978-1-6641-6134-4 (sc)
ISBN: 978-1-6641-6135-1 (hc)
ISBN: 978-1-6641-6133-7 (e)

Print information available on the last page

Rev. date: 03/04/2021

Dedication page:

To all the colorful babes
of the world.

Light skinned

Brown skinned

Some have straight long hair

Dark skinned

Red skinned

Some have kinky coils up there

Yellow toned

Big boned

Some have freckles too

Brown eyes

Grey eyes

Some have blue eyes it's true!

Some are big and tall

Some are short and small

Some are big and short

Or tall and thin

Some eat whole food

Some eat soul food

Some are women and some are men

Afrocentric

Or uniquely intricate

All have their own special style

Some grin broadly

Some smirk oddly

Some have a big bright smile

No matter how different

No matter how far

The lesson is clear and simple

We were all gorgeously and
wonderfully made

And we are ALL the same KIND of people.

The End

About the Author

Janace L Griffin is an alumni of North Carolina Agricultural and Technical State as well as Liberty University were she obtained her Bachelors degree in Psychology and Masters in Human Services Family and Marriage Counseling. She is a member of Sigma Gamma Rho Sorority Incorporated and currently pursuing her PhD in Philosophy of Psych at Liberty Univ. She resides in East Carolina with her spouse, son and mother. She enjoys photography, reading and writing.

Printed in the United States
by Baker & Taylor Publisher Services